I0596293

MAVETH
BLOODSPORT

Maveth: Bloodsport is a work of fiction. References to real people, events, establishments, organizations, or locales are intended only to provide the sense of authenticity and are use fictitiously. All other characters, all incidents, dialogue are drawn from the author's imagination and are not to be seen as real.

Copyright © 2020 by Ty'Ron W. C. Robinson II. All rights reserved.

Published by Dark Titan Entertainment.

Also available in e-book format.

Dark Titan Universe is a branch of Dark Titan Entertainment.

First Printing 2020. Printed in the U.S.A.

ISBN: 978-1-7353154-0-9

darktitanentertainment.com

WORKS BY TY'RON W. C. ROBINSON II

<u>BOOKS</u>

DARK TITAN UNIVERSE SAGA

MAIN SERIES

Dark Titan Knights
The Resistance Protocol
Tales of the Scattered
Tales of the Numinous
Day of Octagon

<u>Forthcoming</u>

Crossbreed
Heaven's Called
The Resistance/Protectors War

SPIN-OFFS

In A Glass of Dawn: The Casebook of Travis Vail
Maveth: Bloodsport

<u>Forthcoming</u>

The Curse of The Mutant-Thing
Trail of Vengeance
War of The Thunder Gods

THE HAUNTED CITY SAGA

The Legendary Warslinger: The Haunted City I
Battle of Astolat: A Haunted City Prequel (KOBO Exclusive)
Redemption of the Lost: The Haunted City II
Consequences of the Suffering: The Haunted City III (Forthcoming)

SYMBOLUM VENATORES

Symbolum Venatores: The Gabriel Kane Collection
Hod: A Symbolum Venatores Book
Symbolum Venatores: War of The Two Kingdoms (Forthoming)

OTHER BOOKS

Lost in Shadows: A Novel
Lost in Shadows: Remastered
Accounts of The Dead Days
The Book of The Elect
Hallow Sword: Cursed(KOBO Exclusive)
Dark Titan Omnibus: Volume 1
The Extended Age Omnibus
Frightened!: The Beginning (Forthcoming)
EverWar Universe: Knights & Lords (Forthcoming)
Dark Titan Omnibus: Volume 2 (Forthcoming)

A DARK TITAN UNIVERSE SAGA SPIN-OFF

MAVETH BLOODSPORT

TY'RON W. C. ROBINSON II

DARK TITAN UNIVERSE

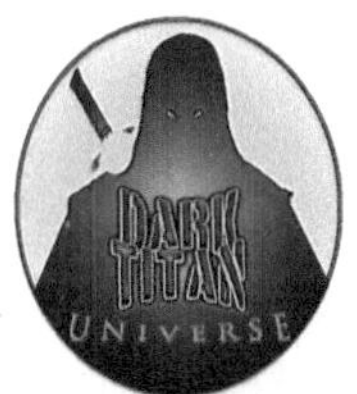

"Your first mission is given, Maveth. See you do it well."

"I will, and I will receive payment as promised."

"Yes. Your payment will come in full."

The phone hanged up. Standing in his armory, Danton Thomas prepared himself for the mission. An assassination contract. Danton grabbed his weapons of choice and last, he grabbed his sword. One used casually during his missions. Danton was set and placed his helmet on, giving him the appearance of a Black Ops grim reaper. His demeanor and presence is what gave him the name: Maveth, the Death-Bringer.

First order of business is meeting with one of the heads of Glasco, Inc. Danton traveled to their headquarters in Germany. There, he met the woman dressed in green and black. Marion Von Eldric. A woman's whose confidence matches the men around the organization. Sometimes, overcoming them in precision and ethic.

"Great you've made it in time."

"Likewise." Danton said. "I was told Ezekiel McKnight would be speaking with me. Not you of all people."

"McKnight is currently occupied with another meeting. You will speak with me and you will listen."

"Will I now?"

"If you want your payment delivered to you in full."

"Fair enough, Lady Von Eldric." Danton nodded.

"Follow me, Mr. Thomas."

Danton walked with Marion into the headquarters. Inside were many employees, dressed in scientific apparel with others pertaining to military services. Danton is impressed with the number of people working within the headquarters.

"I wonder how you've managed to acquire such a number of employees under your wings."

"We have our methods of persuasion."

"Didn't use any of them on me, did you?" Danton said smirking.

"You're a natural charmer when it comes to it." Marion said. "No reason for us to try and please you."

"There are other ways to please me." Danton said, staring hard into Marion's eyes.

"Don't try it." She demanded. "Not here at least."

Entering her primary office of the headquarters, Danton looked up at the board on the wall, seeing several headshot photos of various individuals. He approached the board, staring at the photos while Marion sat behind her desk, pulling out a file from the drawer.

"Who are these people?"

"Traitors to Glasco." Marion said. "Traitors to be found and put to death."

"And that's why you contacted me? To eliminate these traitors of yours?"

"Not all of them. Just one. For now."

"Which of these is the one you want me to kill? The fellow man or the lovely woman?"

Marion opened the file, pulling out another photo, sliding it toward Danton. He grabbed the photo from the desk.

"And who might this be?"

"His name is Austin Harris. He was one of us before he went rogue and aligned himself with T.I.T.A.N."

"Oh. I see it now." Danton said. "He went to work for the competition."

"I wouldn't call it competition."

"So, what would you call it? Because from my point of view, it's always a competition. Which organization can retrieve new information on these rising heroes of the world?"

"You know of them? These figures rising up all over the world?"

"I may keep to myself, but I am fully aware of what's going on in the world. I've heard stories of these kinds of heroes. Coming out of the blue and saving the innocent. There's all kinds of them."

"And you don't find it strange how they're suddenly showing up at once. As if it was destined to happen like this?"

"I believe every moment has its purpose. The purpose of these heroes is yet to be revealed and I know for certain that my future will have a part in their purpose."

"Like what? You're going to join them and save the world?"

"No. I'm going to eliminate them one by one. If there are heroes, then someone must be the villain. All in the balance."

Marion nodded. Sensing Danton was speaking the truth concerning himself and the heroes. She understood him well and knew him well enough to determine where he'll end up in the future and she was happy of it.

"Now, where is the present location of this Austin Harris?" Danton asked calmly.

"We're been receiving Intel concerning his whereabouts." Marion said, handing Danton a map. He gazed at the map for several seconds.

"I've heard of this city."

"That's good. So, you know where it is and how to get there."

"Of course. I've done a few missions there. Dealing with their criminal underworld."

"How soon can you get there?"

"By any means." Danton declared with confidence emitting from his voice.

Marion nodded, standing up behind her desk. She extended her hand toward Danton. He looked and stared.

"Then, you know what to do."

"Yes, ma'am." Danton said, shaking her hand. "I do."

Danton walked toward the exit and stopped, turning back toward Marion.

"Since Retropolis is far from here. I will stay at a local place tonight and leave in the morning."

"Do what you must." Marion said. "As long as everything goes according to plan. That's what I care about."

"I see." Danton said, leaving the office.

Danton went to a local place of residence, purchased by him some time ago during one of his earlier missions. The place was of a small home in the wilderness. The wilderness and the quietness of the land pleased Danton and he enjoyed it. Later in the night as Danton was preparing for his rest, a knock came from the door. Danton wasn't sure who could know where he'll be, grabbed his sword as he approached the door. He opened it and saw Marion.

"You are prepared everywhere you go." She said, staring at the sword in his hand.

"I have to be." Danton said. "It keeps me focused."

Marion's presence confused Danton. He looked around in case the premises were crowded with Glasco soldiers or those involved with V.A.U.L.T. he was certain her presence wasn't no accident or test to prove his loyalty.

"I have to ask, why are you here?"

"May I come in?"

"Why?"

"I'll tell you why I'm here if you would let me in."

Danton thought to himself. He nodded and allowed Marion to enter. Shutting the door, Marion looked around the home. It is a casual home. Nothing out of the ordinary except for the complete layout of weapons on the floor next to the bed.

"Was all of this here already or did you bring it with you?"

"Little bit of both."

"Very well." Marion said. "We chose well to contact you."

"Don't concern yourself with this Austin Harris. Once I reach Retropolis, I will find him and eliminate him. Problem will be solved."

Danton walked up to Marion, drinking a glass of whiskey. His presence intimidated Marion. She was out of her element and there were no Glasco soldiers to protect her. She knew it and Danton knew.

"Now that you're inside, why are you here?" Danton asked.

"I came for another reason."

"What is this reason you've chosen to come?"

"I wouldn't call it another briefing. More like an intact deal between you and I."

"What kind of deal were you thinking?"

Marion kissed Danton. She backed away as Danton processed the kiss and the intent of Marion's presence. He nodded slowly. Taking in a breath.

"This was your kind of deal?"

"You could say that."

Danton smiled and grabbed Marion roughly by her waist. Kissing her. Danton tossed her atop his bed, kissing her more and more. They ripped off each other's clothing. Now, fully naked and on top of the bed. Danton pleasured Marion as she moaned and screamed in enjoyment. Danton treated Marion's body as if it was his own and Marion had done the same.

After their rough intercourse, Danton prepared himself to leave as the sun was starting to rise. Marion watched him dress in his armor and gear. It turned her own watching him sharpen his swords and load his guns. She smiled as he did every act.

"How can you carry all of it?"

"Because there's no other way to keep it close." Danton said.

Danton was prepared and ready. Marion dressed herself and left the residence. Kissing Danton as she left. Danton was set and headed out, traveling toward the airport. He walked toward his plane, codenamed *04191*. Danton entered the plane as the pilot was informed by Marion earlier. The plane, a dark gray in nature took off from the airport. Making its way to Retropolis.

The morning of Retropolis is somewhat bright and gloomy. Civilians move about on their daily routine. Danton stood atop a roof, overlooking a site dedicated to the faithful leaders of the city. Danton held his binoculars and scoped the area. Searching, Danton spotted Austin. He nodded.

"There's the man."

Danton placed his finger on the earpiece while watching Austin stand with men wearing black with the T.I.T.A.N. emblem on their uniforms. On the other end of the earpiece speaking to Danton is Marion.

"I've found him."

"Can you get the shot?" Marion asked.

"Not from this angle." Danton said. "There are too many T.I.T.A.N. agents standing near him. As if they're aware."

"Aware of what?"

"As if they know someone has been sent to assassinate their prize."

"They can't possibly know that. Unless we have more traitors in our camp."

"That is a job for yourself and your associates." Danton declared. "Leave Austin to me and only to me."

"Can I be sure of this?"

"After that night we shared and the fact that I'm standing on a rooftop in Retropolis, overlooking the man whom you want dead, yes, you can be sure of it. Austin Harris will be dead by the day's end."

"See that it is."

Danton could hear the silent on the other end of the earpiece. Marion had hung up. Danton smirked faintly as he gazed over, watching Austin standing around the surrounding agents.

Danton continued to follow Austin throughout the city as he made movements. Austin led Danton to a warehouse outside of the city limits. Danton scouted the warehouse, noticing the location was owned by someone within Retropolis or Mass City, its sister city. Danton watched while Austin entered the warehouse with the T.I.T.A.N. agents.

"Come nightfall, I will be prepared."

Danton suited up in his gear and uniform, last equipping his masked helmet and sheathing his sword. Danton has become Maveth. Running down toward the warehouse from the nearby cliff, Maveth scouted the warehouse's landscape. He moved near one of the shattered windows, peeking through. Inside, Maveth could see Austin and the T.I.T.A.N. agents. Standing around a table with a laptop and several suitcases.

"Packages must be important." Maveth remarked. "Wonder what they could be hiding."

Maveth moved throughout the area, finding a way into the warehouse from prying eyes. As he made his way in, he noticed several T.I.T.A.N. agents were heading outside with rifles. Intrigued and relieved, he knew what they were setting up. A perimeter.

"Good timing. I made it in."

Maveth hid behind several crates, all stamped with the T.I.T.A.N. emblem as a few moved over into another room of the warehouse with the Glasco, Inc. stamp and the V.A.U.L.T. emblem. Maveth was on point and at the precise location.

"I should take him out." Maveth said. "But, before that is done, I must rid his surroundings of these agents. Keep the area clear for my kill."

Maveth watched, counting five T.I.T.A.N. agents standing around Austin at the table. Maveth counted closely and planned his move of attack. His plan has worked before and he was confident it would work well again. Maveth nodded.

"Time to make my move."

Maveth tossed a smoke grenade near the agents. The grenade bounced with a tipping sound of metal hitting concrete. The grenade rolled toward the agents. The agents heard the sound and they spot the grenade. Stopping its rolling. The grenade sounded off a clicking beep and exploded. Covering the area in thick grey smoke. Through the smoke, Maveth moved swiftly, killing the agents one by one with his sword. Austin ducked down underneath the table. Austin glinted through the smoke and saw the agents falling dead. The smoke cleared and only Maveth was standing in the room amongst the dead agents. Austin bolted from the table, running toward the door. Maveth threw a blade, hitting Austin in his calf. Austin fell, yelling in pain and gaining the attention of the sniper agents.

"Better if you kept your agony down." Maveth said.

"Who are you?!"

"I'm here to kill you."

"For what reason?"

"You're a traitor to Glasco, Inc. They sent me here to make sure you didn't deliver any details to T.I.T.A.N. and by the look of this place, you have done so."

"Only for good reason did I betray them!"

"It's not my call and it's not my problem."

Austin begged Maveth to spare his life. Maveth nodded and shot Austin clear in the head. Maveth placed his gun into its holster and sighed.

"Mission accomplished." Maveth said.

Outside, he could hear the sirens coming toward the warehouse. Maveth moved out as the Retropolis Police rammed through the doors. Running in were Detectives Justine Copeland and Cash Hankinson. Behind them entered Commissioner James Austin. They saw the bodies of the agents with Austin lying on the floor. The used grenade sitting amongst them.

"What the hell happened here?" Commissioner Austin asked.

"We'll find out soon." Justine said. "Give us a little time, boss."

While more officers entered the warehouse, Maveth was

standing atop the cliff from which he came. He nodded once more, removing his mask helmet. He took a moment to breathe and contacted Marion through the earpiece.

"Report Maveth."

"Mission has been fulfilled. Austin Harris is dead."

"No traces back to Glasco?"

"None. Everything is secure. As planned."

"Excellent." Marion said with gladness in her voice. "Return to base and you will have your payment."

"Wonderful." Danton responded, hanging up the call.

Danton turned around to leave the area and felt a disturbing presence within nearby. Danton slowly decided to turn back to the warehouse and when he did, he saw someone. Standing across from him on the other end of the high round. He saw the figure with a cloak and hood. Its eyes glowed through the night sky and the figure wielded a sword. Danton and the figure stared down one another for several seconds. Danton smirked, realizing the figure's identity. Putting on his masked helmet, Maveth raised his sword, pointing it at the figure.

"Soon." Maveth declared, leaving the area. "I will return to this city. For a bigger prize."

MAVETH: BLOODSPORT

I

TAKE THE CALL

On a bright clear day, Danton Thomas fired some rounds from his M4 on his private range. After taking several more shots, blowing the head of the dummy clear off, his cell phone rang. Lowering the firearm and gazing down at the table behind him, seeing the phone blinking.

"Danton."

"It's Marion. You know why I've called."

"I do. What's the mission?"

"Come by the headquarters as per usual for briefing and I'll tell you everything as scheduled. Get yourself ready."

"I'm on my way."

Danton left the range and entered his weaponry. Glancing at the arsenal around him before approaching the closet and opening it, revealing his tactical suit of Kevlar. Known as the *Death-Bringer* armor. He put on the armor and grabbed his weapons of choice before grabbing his sword last. He left the armory and his homestead.

Sometime later, he arrived at the Glasco, Inc. Headquarters in Germany. The same location as his previous briefings for missions. Upon entering the building, he was approached by Marion von Eldric. She greeted Danton with a smile, yet not a friendly one at that.

"Good of you to arrive."

"I'm here for business. Now, what is the mission?"

"This way."

Unlike Danton's last encounter with the place, there were more military personnel than before. Danton's sense of awareness increased as they walked down the hallway toward the office. They entered Marion's office and she shut the door, walking behind her desk. Danton sat down, removing his helmet and placing it on the desk, waiting.

"The mission, Marion."

"Don't rush me."

Marion reached over to the bookshelf, raising up a folder, sliding it toward Danton. He grabbed the folder and saw what was inside, reading carefully.

"A Don?" Danton questioned.

"Yes. One we've been looking for, for quite a while."

"And you finally found him. How so?"

"We have connections."

"I'm not buying the proposed fact that some organization tipped this guy off to you and your militia pals. This type of mission had to have been done by someone on their own. Someone in higher authority."

Marion nodded.

"There was someone who told us. Plainly simple."

"Where was this Don sighted?"

"Enigma City."

Danton chuckled.

"Enigma City? I have a feeling who might've told you now."

"Who do you have in mind?"

Danton paused. Shaking his head and closing the folder.

"Doesn't matter. I'll find this Don and report back to you as planned."

Maveth went and left from Marion's office. Taking the trip similar to the previous ones, Maveth grabbed his gear and hopped into the plane. While in the air, Danton took the moment to think on the matter at hand. Another mission. More pay. More solitude. Elsewhere, Marion was on the phone speaking to an individual who's searching for a mercenary to hire. Marion responded to the caller by stating she's knows one and more than the one.

Maveth arrived in Enigma City during the midday. Scouting the city, seeing it's much cleaner and slick than Retropolis. The scenery bothered Maveth to the point where he entered the building to avoid looking out at the glistening cityscape. The cleanliness irked him.

"This city is no place for me."

Reading up on the files, he learned the Don was kept at a homestead near the outskirts of the city. Danton made his travels to the outskirts by way of a vehicle which was provided to him by V.A.U.L.T. Driving out of the city, he saw what appeared to be a flying blue and white streak past ahead of him in the sky.

"He's around these parts. Figures much."

Making it to the outskirts, Danton spotted the homestead, guarded by a dozen armed guards. Four of which stood in watchtowers around the wooden home. Danton prepared himself, putting on his helmeted mask. He stepped out of the car from a distance. His sword were set and his firearms loaded. He snuck into the region, immediately taking out the four watchmen by slashing their throats. He moved from tower to tower by the cable lines connecting them to the home. After the watchmen were taken out, he moved to the ground and began running through the armed guards with his sword. Others he shot with his silencer pistol. Maveth moved with speed to take out the guard and he was finished. He approached the front door of the home, kicking it down to see there was no one inside.

"The hell is this guy?"

Maveth entered and from behind him stood someone else. Another mercenary who through Maveth's mind off the mission for a split second. Standing before him, the mercenary wore complete armor and Kevlar of white and silver. His face covered with a helmeted mask of their own. Maveth knew them and he knew them well.

"Gunbaine." Maveth said. "What are you doing here?"

"I could ask you the same thing."

"Skipping A.B.'s orders for her Enforcement?"

"She knows why I'm here and the purpose of it."

"Perhaps, you should focus on those matters and leave the mercenary duties to me."

"And why would I do that? Leave all the fancy jobs to you and I deal with the scraps."

"This is my mission. My duty."

"I don't see it that way. Neither does V.A.U.L.T."

"What do you know of them? Has A.B. spoken with you about this?"

"Marion informed her of the plans. The Enforcement was planned to be a part of this. However, the members saw opportunities which didn't sit well with A.B.'s orders. She's talked with a lot of us about V.A.U.L.T. The two of us are just a few who are informed of their secrets."

"What of the Don?"

"A ploy. To get you to realize you're not the only mercenary around. Besides, it was a test."

"A test for what cause? To see my loyalty?"

"To see if you were ready for the reveal."

"Where's Marion?"

"I was just going to meet us. I'm sure you'll want to come."

Maveth walked past Gunbaine swiftly. Gunbaine scoffed under his breath, placing his pistol in the holster as Maveth walked away.

"Do you know where to go?" Gunbaine wondered.

"I'll see you there, Smalls."

II

INTRODUCING THE CHALLENGERS

Marion contacted Danton, Gunbaine, and the others, signaling them to arrive at the V.A.U.L.T. headquarters. Upon Danton's arrival, he saw more soldiers around the facility and they were shook. Their firearms up and ready to fire. Inside, Danton saw Marion standing in the midst of other mercenaries.

"What is all of this?" Danton asked.

"I see you've made it." Marion replied. "Good. Now, I can tell you all everything you must know."

Danton took a look at the others inside the facility. Some he knew. Others he didn't. The mercenaries inside the facility besides Maveth and Gunbaine were Tessa Balthazar the Treasure Huntress, the Exchange Force, Cartavious Cage, Deadon the Commando, Lynch the Hunter, Kane the Mercenary, The Bandit, and Cain. Marion continued speaking to the mercenaries concerning their purpose to being inside the facility. As she talked, Danton was focused.

"There is a prize at stake." Marion said. "Only those such as yourselves are capable of retrieving it. For it will bring to you a bigger future and more opportunities to come. Now, the rules are simple, during this obstacle course, defeat all of the other mercenaries and come out on top. Although, no killing. There are other jobs to offer."

"For what gives?!" Lynch the Hunter uttered.

"Don't concern yourself, brother." Kane the Mercenary replied. "We have our ways to get around it. You know."

"Ah."

"I hope you'll all have some fun with this." Marion concluded. "I know you will."

Everyone talked among themselves while Marion left their presence, returning to her office, however, Danton saw her and followed. Lynch and Kane gazed around at the other mercenaries, scoffing. They turned to see Tessa walking past them.

"Where are you going?" Lynch asked.

"None of your concern."

"Listen." Kane said. "We'll all in this game together. How about you join us and make it to the finish."

"I'll make it on my own."

"Don't do anything you'll regret, woman." Lynch said, stepping forward.

"Is that a threat?"

"Depends on your decision."

Tessa turned and walked away. Lynch didn't take it kindly and went to follow, only to be stopped by Kane.

"Not right now. We'll get to her later."

Marion reached her office door and Danton came from behind as the door opened.

"What is all of this?!"

"All of what?"

"This mission with the Don? It was all a ploy to get me here? To participate in this game you've constructed?"

"In a manner of speaking."

"You played me like a fool!"

"I did not. This is an opportunity greater than the mission you were given. What could be better than finding a crime lord other than a game. A game of mercenaries. All out for the same prize."

"What is the prize you've promised them?"

"I can't give you that information. Classified."

"Classified? From me? After all I've done?"

"Defeat the other mercs and win the game. You'll find out that way."

"You said no killing. I only know how to kill when there's opposition in my way."

"Then, you'll have to find a solution to avoid slaughtering them. Besides, not all of them will be a problem for you. Just a few."

"I don't work well with others."

"You and Gunbaine turned out well." Marion noted. "Seems you two didn't go and kill each other in Enigma City."

"We have a mutual respect."

"I'm sure you do after your pact in Retropolis fell through."

"It didn't fall through." Danton said. "We just came across an enemy who knew us well. Very well."

"And I'm sure you want another opportunity to make it right. For yourself and your pride."

"I'll get my chance one day."

"Do yourself a favor and keep your eyes on this game. Win it and maybe, you'll get that chance. Lose the game and you may not. Your choice."

Danton nodded with thoughts running through his mind. He turned to the door and looked back to Marion at the desk.

"Where's the first phase of this game taking place?"

"In Manchester. There is a ball taking place. It'll be filled with wealthy patrons of course. I'll be sending you and the mercs out there. You'll find out why when you do."

"Will it require killing one of these patrons?"

"Perhaps. Maybe. Who's to tell."

Danton smirked and walked out of the office. Marion sat still with a grin on her face, overlooking a file containing information on all the mercenaries.

Danton walked back out into the front, seeing the mercenaries still in place, talking to each other. Tessa was nowhere to be seen. Lynch and Kane stood against the all, speaking with several V.A.U.L.T. soldiers. While, walking to the outside, Deadon stepped in front of him, measuring his uniform.

"We're a lot alike." Deadon said.

"In appearance, yes." Danton replied. "However, in skill, we've yet to determine he case."

"Perhaps, in this game, if we cross paths, we'll find out."

"You don't want to test that theory."

"It's my job to test all things. Prove them to see if they're indeed fact."

"The fact will become your end if you continue to speak in this manner toward me."

"Throwing out threats already and the game hasn't even begun."

"If you want to stay in the game, you'll keep quiet."

Deadon nodded, stepping away. Danton walked outside and left the headquarters. Returning to his homestead as always. He rested for the remainder of the day. The other mercenaries had places prepared for them. Similar to Danton's stead. The following morning, the mercenaries were contacted individually and were privately taken to the airport, where they were flown off to England.

Now in Manchester, the mercenaries gathered at a facility owned by V.A.U.L.T. themselves. Within the briefing room, Marion arrived and instructed the mercenaries on the details of the game and what it features. She began to tell them of the ball later that night. Speaking that the mercenaries should prepare themselves for the night. Find a way to blend in with the crowd of patrons and visitors. The objective of this part of the game will be told when nightfall comes around. The mercenaries went to their own places of stay for the rest of the day. Preparing themselves for the ball in any way they can.

Danton sat in his room, mediating. A knock echoed from the door, jolting him from his meditation. He stood up and opened it, seeing Marion as she walked in.

"Why have you come?" Danton asked. "Why visit me?"

"Because I wanted to see how you're doing. Before you head out to the ball."

"A ball you orchestrated. For your little game."

"This is only a game fit for mercenaries. You are one of them. One of the best."

"And you expect me to find the patron and win this portion of the game?"

"I know you will."

"Have you spoken to the other mercs? Besides Smalls?"

"I've spoken with Balthazar. She seems thrilled to be involved in such a game."

"The girl's a treasure seeker. Not a mercenary."

"She has skill." Marion referenced. "Very precise in her craft."

"I've heard from those she's stolen from."

"And none of them are here to capture her. Besides, isn't that a task only fit for a mercenary?"

"I've never had to opportunity of confronting her. She's too young for her own good."

"Maybe you can talk to her. Put some sense into her."

"Better you than me."

"You better than me to talk to her."

Danton sighed.

"Why'd you really come?"

"I've come to tell you it's better if you go into the ball incognito. You don't want the people to see a fully dressed mercenary scurrying around the ball."

"You want me to wear a two-piece suit and join in?"

"Only if you want to find the patron quietly."

Danton nodded with a smirk. He approached the door and Marion knew what he meant as she walked past him.

"I guess I'll be seeing you at the ball tonight?" Danton asked.

"You'll find out when you show up."

Marion left as Danton closed the door. He turned around and exhaled quietly before returning to his mediation. Upon mediating again, he glanced over toward the chair against the wall where his Maveth mask sat, staring at him. He gazed into the eyes of the helmet. Feeling the urge growing.

Elsewhere in Manchester, the mercenaries were ready. Yet, only a few of them were visited by Marion in similar fashion as Maveth. Once nightfall had approached, Danton exited his residence, wearing a suit with no tie. He approached the front, finding a vehicle waiting for him. He scoffed.

"Figures much."

Danton entered the car as he drove off. Inside the car sat Marion facing him. He laughed within himself, shaking his head.

"I wasn't aware we'll be arriving together." Danton said.

"It's all for the diversion."

"And the other mercs? How will they be arriving?"

"Each one has their own style. They'll do what they know."

They arrive at the ball, seeing it crowded with people of Manchester. Danton and Marion enter together and quickly, Danton scanned the area, seeing Tessa standing on the second-floor balcony. On the other side were Kane and Lynch, dressed in suits of their own. Passing by Danton and Marion were five individuals, he looked at them and recognized who they were without question.

"Didn't know the Exchange Force knew how to dress well." Danton said.

"Everyone has their ways." Marion replied. "I'm sure you're looking for the patron."

"I am. Where is he?"

"He?" Marion questioned with a grin.

She pointed in front of them toward a woman. From her appearance, she had to be someone of authority within Manchester. An experienced woman in the political field. She was the patron. Danton saw her and how she conducted herself to the others.

"Who is she?"

"Someone important to this city."

"What is the objective of all this?"

"You'll need to get her out of here."

"Get her out? For what purpose?"

"This place is about to get a little loud."

"What are you talking about, Marion? Tell me."

"Get her out now. I'll meet with you back at your residence."

Marion left the ball, leaving Danton standing in the room confused. He turned toward the patron and approached her. She looked at him with questions.

"You don't know me, ma'am. But, I've been informed to escort you out of here."

"Escort me out? For what cause?"

"I'm not certain. However, trust me and I can assure your safety."

Before she could answer, Deadon burst through eh doors, guns blazing. The people panicked upon the sound of the firing, running amok inside the room. Danton held the patron down and ran with her to the outside.

"What is going on?!" She asked.

"Stay out here. I'll find out what's happening inside."

Danton returned to the room, seeing only Deadon standing, facing him. Two machine guns in his hands.

"The Death-Bringer in a suit?" Deadon joked. "What has the world come to."

"This is how you come to a ball? Shoot up everyone. Aren't you aware of the patron?"

"I am. But, here's the thing. I'm a mercenary. Like you. I kill who I'm paid to kill. Same as you. However, it seems our deals have crossed paths. I saw you take the woman outside. I've been sent to kill her."

"I've been told to protect her."

"Have you? Seems our paths are crossed after all."

Danton jolted his arms and out of the sleeves appeared two pistols. Sleek and precise in size. Deadon scoffed at the sight of them.

"Clever man. You believe those peashooters will outperform my rounds?"

"Only way to find out, Commando." Danton replied. "Your move."

"My move it is."

Deadon fired the first shots as Danton dodged them with his speed. Firing back, Deadon bolted to the opposite wall of the room, taking more shots as Danton continued. Deadon fired back and the two mercenaries sat still, waiting for the other to attack.

"Tired already?" Deadon mocked. "It isn't your style, Death-Bringer!"

"The night is still young, boy."

On the opposite side of the room, Bandit ran in and started shooting toward the people near the doors. Gunbaine bolted in and started firing toward Bandit, who ducked underneath the nearby counter of wine and champagne. Gunbaine paused his shots.

"Why are you killing them?"

"This is a moment of fun for men like us. Take some shots and enjoy the night."

"I can't let you kill them. They are not our target."

"I pick my own targets, Smalls."

On the second floor, Tessa is being harassed by Lynch and Kane. She ran down the corridor to avoid them. They followed as she entered a room and shut the door. Kane ran into the door, yet it was too dense for his weight. Lynch shook his head with shame, pointing toward Kane's glock on his side.

"Think wisely, man." Lynch suggested.

Kane looked at his firearm and gestured with a nod humor toward Lynch. Lynch kicked the door open and they ran in. The room itself was only a lounge room. Two sofas against the opposite walls facing each other. A small table set with a lamp and magazines and books of British Literature. Lynch kicked the table.

"The hell did she go?!"

"She couldn't have gone far, man." Kane said, running to the opened window. "Hey, you think she jumped?"

Lynch approached the window and looked out, only to see the pavement of the ground. Tessa was nowhere in sight. Lynch shook his head again, turning away from the window as Kane closed it with a slam.

"She's still here on the property." Lynch uttered. "All of us are."

"That brings the question. We're still hearing the shootout downstairs. That was Gunbaine, Deadon, Bandit, and Death-Bringer. Where are the others?"

"Who?"

"The Exchange Force, Cage, and the big guy?"

"They're here. Somewhere. Maybe they'll find Tessa for us. Then, we can relish her in our own ways."

They continued to search the estate and turn corners down the hallways of the second floor. After their third turn, they saw five figures facing them from the other end of the hallway. Kane jolted, raising his gun.

"The hell are they?"

"The Exchange Force." Lynch said. "Let's clean up the competition."

"Absolutely!"

Lynch and Kane fired toward the Force, who have removed their casual attire for their armored gear. The Hunter and The Mercenary fired down at the force as two of its members rushed toward them with swords. Downstairs continually Maveth and Deadon fire rounds as Gunbaine and Bandit do the same. Gunbaine ran out into the firefight between the Death-Bringer and the commando, ducking down and taking a shot toward Deadon before diving behind the counter, directly in Maveth's presence. Maveth wasn't keen on seeing Gunbaine at the moment and neither was Gunbaine.

"Can't you see I'm busy!"

"As am I."

"You wouldn't have come over here without some kind of plan."

"Where's the patron?"

"I got her out. She's clear."

"So, what do we do about these two?"

Bandit walked out, getting Deadon's attention. Bandit held his hands up with guns in tow. He approached Deadon calmly.

"I'm on you side here." Bandit said. "Let's take these two out and return to the base. Clear the competition."

Deadon thought for a second and agreed with a nod. The two turned toward the counter and shot it up. Maveth and Gunbaine held their own to avoid the incoming rounds. Outside of the estate, Tessa moved stealthy to get out of the land. Before she could, she was grabbed by Cage. His smile was terrifying and his eyes were wide. Tessa struggled, but Cage was too strong for someone very lean.

"I need another mark on my list!"

"I'll mark you up!" Tessa said, kicking Cage back.

He let her go and grabbed her again. She continued kicking him and quickly stopped as Cage turned around, seeing Cain standing. Cain grabbed Cage by his neck and tossed him against the estate wall. Tessa backed away slowly as Cain saw Cartavious was knocked out from the impact. Cain turned toward Tessa, helping her to her feet. Tessa was in fear of Cain for his large size and intimidating presence. His eyes showed no pupils and his mask summoned fear.

"Go." Cain said. "Make sure you return to your residence safely."

"Thank you." Tessa replied.

"No need."

Tessa made her way back to her residence. Cain entered the estate, hearing the gunfire from both the first and second floors. Cain moved upstairs, finding Lynch and the other Kane fighting the Exchange Force. Cain stomped the ground, quaking it. The Force stumbled as did Lynch and Kane. They turned, seeing Cain standing still.

"Shit." Kane said.

"The hell is he supposed to be?" Lynch asked. "Beast wanna-be?"

"Return to your residences." Cain said. "This part of the game is over."

"Who are you to give us orders?" Lynch asked.

Cain ran with superhuman speed and shoulder tackled Lynch to the wall and turned to the others. Hoping they'll fight back, yet they chose not to and left the second floor to save their own lives. Cain looked down at Lynch, who's grunting in pain and walked back downstairs toward the ball room.

Once Cain arrived downstairs, he saw the gunfire between Maveth and Gunbaine against Deadon and Bandit. Cain knew he couldn't just run in the middle of the gunfire. He shrugged his shoulders and reached into his belt pocket, pulling out small pellets. He tossed them into the room and they explode upon hitting the floor, stumbling the four armed men. They looked over, seeing Cain as he tossed another pellet into the room. This time a smoke bomb. As the smoke took over the room, Cain measured the four men and nodded.

"This portion of the game is over. Now, onto the next."

After Cain finished speaking, police sirens echoed from the outside, causing the mercenaries to escape quickly. Once they were outside and away from the estate, Maveth looked around and only Gunbaine was in his sights. Deadon, Bandit, and Cain were gone.

III

UNIFICATION OF SKILLS

The next morning, Danton trained in his residence before leaving Manchester. The mercenaries were taken onto the plane and brought to a private island. Owned by a wealthy partaker who's funding the game. Marion gathered the mercenaries together. However, Cartavious Cage was not present among them. As he was defeated by Cain back at the ball.

"This is how this portion works." Marion said. "Each of you will be placed on a particular part of the island, where you all must arrive at the mansion. Once you're inside, you must find the briefcase. Silver, little chromed touch. Grab it and bring it to the copper. On your own, no team ups concerning the case."

"Pardon," Lynch uttered. "If I may?"

"Go ahead."

"You're saying basically on this island, anything goes."

"Anything besides killing. There's no need to kill each other when other opportunities await."

Lynch grinned, glaring toward Tessa on the other end of the room.

"Good for me."

"What's inside of this case, Marion?" Danton asked. "Sure, it's something important."

"It is. Intel on our competitors."

"Hmm. Which one?"

"You might find out once inside the mansion."

Danton nodded with a grin. Standing back against the wall of the briefing room. The Exchange Force stood quietly. So did Gunbaine, Deadon, Bandit, Tessa, and Cain.

"That is all. You'll all be flown to the island at once."

"And will you also be there?" Danton asked. "To keep your eyes on us?"

"Unfortunately, I have some other business to attend. However, I will be present when the round is over."

"Sure you will."

Marion sent them off and the mercenaries were flown to the island. A place sitting in the middle of the Indian Ocean. Danton observed the island from the air. It seemed familiar to him. He's seen this island before. Been to it once. Danton turned to his front, seeing Deadon sitting.

"We aren't done, Death-Bringer."

"What's your play, Commando?"

"Once we step foot on the island and the round begins, I'm taking you out of this picture."

"That so?"

"Oh, you know it is. I'll be remembered as the victor and the one who eliminated the famed Maveth."

"Don't get cocky yet. The round hasn't begun."

Deadon scoffed. Leaning back in the seat.

"Cockiness sets in the bold."

"Never heard that before. Sounds cheesy."

"You'll see."

The plane landed on the island, particularly on a place designed for air-landings. The mercenaries stepped off the plane. The officials on the plane began to yell toward the mercs to reach the mansion. Danton placed on his helmet and Deadon had him in his sights. Deadon put on his mask, keeping his eyes on Danton.

"My eyes are on you."

"Shut up and reach the mansion." Maveth replied.

In the air above them, several helicopters flew over, heading toward the other end of the island. Danton looked at them closely, seeing an image on their sides.

"T.I.T.A.N.?" Danton said.

The mercenaries ran into the wilderness to reach the mansion. Within the wilderness, Lynch and Kane made it their purpose to chase down Tessa as she jumped up into the trees to reach the mansion. Gunbaine and Bandit went full speed, firing round at each other to only hit the trees. Maveth made his move for the mansion and Deadon walked quietly with his eyes on him. Cain walked calmly through the forest as the rounds flew in front of him and behind. He was not threatened nor caught off guard by the shots. Cain knew the rounds weren't aimed at him, and he didn't care. His only concern was the briefcase. The Exchange Force were scattered on opposite ends of the island, each one making their move to the center. A tactic they've used countless times on missions.

On the other end of the forest, T.I.T.A.N. agents bolted out of the helicopters. A dozen agents in total. All lead by Agent Marshall Henshaw. Gun in hand, dressed in all black besides the white buttoned short-sleeved shirt as he walked toward the mansion. He directed the agents toward the mansion, setting them inside the three-story home. Centered at all points of entry. From the doors to the windows. Agent Henshaw entered the mansion's front doors, kicking them open. Inside the mansion, it was clean. Detailed for a place hidden on a private island in the middle of the ocean.

"Make sure you have your spots! Keep your eyes opened at all times!" Agent Henshaw commanded. "V.A.U.L.T.'s hired operatives will be arriving soon."

Maveth walked through the forest to find the mansion, seeing it's the back end. Above him, Tessa jumped from the trees to the mansion's second floor like a panther, entering one of the second-floor windows. Maveth chuckled at the sight, running toward the back doors. Behind him were Gunbaine and Bandit, still shooting at each other as they went around the corners of the mansion. Deadon walked up to the mansion and entered with Cain following in the distance.

Inside the mansion, Maveth moved around the first floor, seeing the T.I.T.A.N. agents ahead. Hearing their steps from the upper floors. Maveth's ears were keened to his surroundings. He stepped back behind one of the walls of a room. The room itself appeared to be a lounge of sorts, cushioned seats were sitting in front of a counter while sofas were against the walls.

"Shit." Maveth mumbled. "She could've told us."

Two of the agents moved closer to the room and before they could take another step inside, Tessa jumped down from the staircase, kicking the rifles from their hands and tripping them on the ground. The other agents saw her and began firing as she ran back up to the second floor. The agents followed her, giving Maveth the opportunity to make his move. He ran past the staircase, looking at the mansion's interior.

"Who lives here?" He asked himself.

Maveth went down a hallway, leading toward the living room. He went to enter but saw Agent Henshaw with three agents looking around. Maveth backed himself against the wall with his eyes focused not on the agents, but Henshaw.

"Sir, one of the mercenaries was sighted outside."

"Which one?"

"A big guy. Wearing a mask covering his mouth and nose."

"Cain. Make sure you move quietly around him. He's not to be taken lightly."

"Yes sir."

The agents returned to the outside. Maveth held his gun in place, ready to fire. Outside of the mansion, Gunbaine and Bandit continue their shootout, bringing themselves to the attention of the agents. Gunbaine saw them in the distance and they fired toward him. He ran, ducking down behind the brick wall surrounding the pillars of the mansion. Bandit moved to the other end, shooting one agent in the chest.

"These damn fools!" Bandit yelled. "Do you know who you're dealing with?!"

The agents retaliated and fire back toward Bandit, who dodged the coming rounds and returned inside the mansion. Gunbaine looked over at the edge of the wall, seeing the agents rushing into the home chasing Bandit. Gunbaine shook his head.

"We'll see how he'll do."

Inside of the mansion itself, Bandit continually ran as the agent chased and shot at him. Taking every turn possible through the hallways and rooms, he made the move and eventually ran into Deadon, who was prepared for a shootout.

"Why are you standing in here?" Bandit asked.

"To catch these fools off their guard."

The agents bolted into the room, which was a gaming room with arcade machines set on the walls with a pool table to the left of Deadon and Bandit. Deadon raised his firearms. The agents held theirs still. A standoff is in place with Bandit holding his six-shooter aimed at the agents.

"You are to come with us now!" An agent commanded.

"You're giving us orders?" Deadon asked. "We don't work for your kind."

"Either you come with us or we have to shoot!"

Deadon turned to Bandit, who was grinning with excitement.

Deadon moved his focus back to the agents, his fingers on the triggers. He held them tightly and cocked his head. The agents stood firm yet were shivering in a slow fashion. Deadon noticed it and found his mark.

"Very well." Deadon said.

Deadon and Bandit fired at the agents, who only released several shots back, yet, they missed the mark. The agents fell to the floor as Bandit walked over them, shooting them in the chest and head to make sure they're down. Bandit proceeded to look the bodies for anything useful they might have carried around such as money, credit cards, and suchlike. While Bandit was looting, Deadon caught the sound of footsteps outside the door. He paused and raised his hand toward Bandit, who stopped what he was doing.

"What is it?"

"Someone's coming." Deadon said, slowly raising his firearms toward the doorway.

Bandit was ready, standing beside Deadon. Their arms ready to fire as the footsteps inched closer. The sound of them grew with each step. Once the footsteps were loud enough to be near, Deadon and Bandit saw someone standing at the door. The figure was large as it entered the room, looking down at the dead agents.

"Ah." Deadon said. "It's him. The big guy."

Cain had entered the room. He knelt to the agents, closing the eyes. Bandit was confused and attempted to kick one of the agents' bodies. Cain looked up toward him before raising himself up. Bandit held his hands over his head while Deadon was calm and his weapons were down.

"Respect the dead." Cain said. "Whether friend or foe."

"And what if I don't agree with that sentiment?" Bandit asked.

"You won't make it out of here."

"You can't kill us, big man." Deadon said. "Woman's orders. This game is not designed to kill us."

"I'm not going to kill you."

Cain turned back, shutting the door to the room. Bandit raised his guns toward Cain in fear.

"The hell's he doing?" Bandit asked.

"Put your guns down." Deadon said. "Before you do something foolish."

Cain turned back to the mercenaries. His eyes were red. No pupils and the breathing from his mask sent chills down Bandit's body. Chills of fear and chills of the unknown. Bandit held his shooters still, but his hands were sweating, and his fingers were slowly slipping from the triggers.

"Bandit, put your guns down." Deadon said once more. "Put them down!"

"You think you can shoot me?" Cain asked. "Are you up to it?"

"Don't push me." Bandit replied. "I'll do it."

"Bandit, put the damn guns down!" Deadon yelled. "Before he annihilates you."

"No." Cain said. "I'm not going to annihilate him. If he takes the shot, I'm going to curse him."

"You don't think I'll do it?"

"Depends on you. Is your character worth the opportunity at taking the shot? Or are you only in fear because of who stands in front of you?"

"Bandit. For the last time, put down the guns!"

Bandit kept the shooters steady as he breathed heavily. Deadon dropped his firearms and rushed toward Bandit. Cain stood still, waiting for the answer to come forth. Bandit screamed in making a choice and fired the shooters. The rounds pierced Cain's chest armor, bouncing off and falling atop the bodies of the agents. Cain looked down at the bullets. Deadon swiped the shooters from Bandit's hands, however it was too late. Cain stepped forward, rushing into Bandit, slamming him through the wall into another room, which was a guest bedroom. Bandit was on the floor as Cain walked toward him, grabbing him by his head as he tossed him into the walls of the room. Deadon picked up his firearms and fired them, shooting Cain in the back. Cain stood still as the bullets bounced off one by one. Deadon ceased firing as Cain turned around and rushed toward him, doing the same actions he had done to Bandit. The two mercenaries were knocked down, yet they moved slowly and in much pain. Cain sighed and left the room through the opening of the wall.

Elsewhere, as the mansion game went on, Marion sat inside a room with several armed men. The room was dark with dirty walls, appearing to be made of concrete. Only a hanging light from the ceiling and one door. To enter and to exit. The men were not with Marion nor were they affiliated with V.A.U.L.T. They were with the guest who had entered the room. He carried with him a sword and was well-dressed. Marion knew him instantly.

"Mr. Conley." Marion greeted.

"Ms. Eldric. I am delighted you've managed to meet on these terms."

"Any other way doesn't seem truthful."

Conley removed his coat and sat down at the table, facing Marion. His men stood by his side of the room.

"I'm going to call you Conley while we're here." Marion said. "No need to bring up your other name."

"What of that name?"

"It's more for the criminal intent. Something to throw around at other rivals."

Conley nodded.

"But, that's not why we're here."

"No, it is not."

Marion reached over toward her bag, taking out a file. The file came from her office and she slid it over toward Conley, who opened it and saw the pages and the photos which were in place. His eyes went up from the file toward Marion.

"You have these mercs playing in your little game?"

"What's the problem?"

"Maveth's in this. Why?"

"You know him well?"

"Can't say I don't. We've crossed paths very recently. However, I thought The Swordman had gotten to him. Sent him off to Pegasus or killed him."

"No. He was never captured. Truthfully, he made his escape. Gunbaine did as well."

"So, I can see." Conley said, seeing Gunbaine's page in the folder. "So, what's the solution to all of this?"

"Which ever one wins this game will get an opportunity at a bigger prize. The reason you're here right now is because you are familiar with such prizes."

"Basically, in short, you're giving one of these mercs the chance at a high-priority job. Something they would not pass up. Money-wise?"

The doors opened and Conley's men raised their arms up quickly. Marion glared at the doorway with a smirk. Conley turned around to see who was entering as he could hear the footsteps. Marion stood up to greet the incoming visitor.

"Glad you could make it." Marion said.

Entering the room was Kex Kendrick, dressed in his casual white suit and shoes. With him was his assistant Beatrice Mercer. They approached the table and Kex sat on the edge of the table with Marion to his right and Conley to his left. Beatrice stood against the wall, facing Conley's men. Kex began applauding.

"When I was given the call, how could I turn this down."

Marion looked toward Conley and turned back to Kex. The

meeting between the two intrigued her. Never has anyone in their status ever encountered one another. Ever since the appearances of the rising heroes and the *Battle of Retropolis*, things have changed drastically across the world.

"I have to ask, you two haven't met one another before have you?"

"No." Conley said. "We have not. I don't do much work with businessmen of his stature."

"I'm not those men. But, this is the first." Kex replied. "The first of many I hope."

Kex extended his hand toward Conley. Conley stared. Unsure of Kex's nature.

"Are we on familiar terms?" Conley asked. "Concerning the purpose of this meeting?"

"I know of your concerns about your sword-wielding ninja. As I am sure you're familiar about the titagod flying over my city."

"Taltus? He's the one you have a problem with?" Conley questioned. "Now it makes sense. You're one of the ones they brought down during the Battle of Retropolis."

"That I am."

"I take it they're not aware of your status of being a free man once more?" Marion asked.

"They aren't aware of my current whereabouts and I would like to keep it that way."

Conley nodded and shook Kex's hand. Uniting the agreement of the meeting to a complete beginning. Marion was astounded at the work in which could be done with Kex and Conley working together and alongside V.A.U.L.T. An opportunity not fit to bepassed up. A possible unification between them would shake the foundations of the criminal underworld.

"Since you're here, you should take a look at these."

Conley slid the file over to Kex and as soon as he saw the pages and the photos, he was intrigued.

"These are the ones you're working with?" Kex asked Marion.

"They are. See any that intrigue you?"

"Oh, I do. Very much so."

"Now, shall we get to the business at hand?"

"Not without me." A voice said from the door, gaining everyone's attention.

Walking into the room after speaking was A.B., with Lieutenant Gage Hark leading her in. Marion stood up. Conley and Kex were at a loss for words. Hark measured Conley's men and saw Beatrice. He nodded with his AR strapped and held tightly to his chest. The gun was loaded and prepared for any means necessary. Beatrice watched his every move and he did hers. Skilled individuals the two of them are. Gives A.B. and Kex something to show and a means of respect.

"You were in the Force?"

"One time or another."

"Which field may I ask?"

"Marines." Beatrice smirked.

"I can see clearly."

Hark nodded.

"It shows."

A.B. sat at the table, facing Kex, who was confused about jer sudden appearance. He's heard of her workings behind the scenes. Intrigued a bit. Perhaps. She nodded.

"Interesting to see the four of us here as the world continues moving onward."

"Better they do not know why we're here." Conley said. "I take it you're the one who leads that group of baddies."

"Baddies?" Kex asked.

"Enforcement Order." Marion said.

"That unit. Ah, I see."

"I see you've shown the file around, Marion."

"That I did. Conley and Kendrick are certainly interested."

"That's good. I suppose the two of you know anyone in your areas who could be a good fit for my organization."

"I'm sure there are plenty." Kex gestured. "I can make some calls."

"Indeed, you could. How about you, Conley or should I call you J?"

"Conley will do."

"Very well."

"Retropolis is full of opportunists. Crime lords, scavengers, horrors beyond the normal mind of men. I'll make some rounds and send you the Intel. Hell, Pegasus is full of choices for you. Might as well head over there sometime and check out what is available."

"Excellent. But, let's get back to the matter at hand."

"Certainly." Conley replied. "Kex?"

"Absolutely." Kex grinned, handing the file back to Marion.

"Then, let us begin." Marion grinned.

Back at the mansion, Tessa ran past several T.I.T.A.N. agents chasing her. Downstairs on the first floor, Cain walked, casually knocking down agents as the rounds bounce off his chest, arms, and back. On the second floor, Maveth moved through the agents, as he had warned them not to get in his way. After slewing them, he found himself staring off with Agent Henshaw, whose gun was set on Maveth's head.

"Death-Bringer. Figured we would meet again."

"Henshaw, you do not understand what's happening here. This is all a game set up by V.A.U.L.T."

"That right? Then, where are the V.A.U.L.T. soldiers? The crew? The soldiers? The agents? Why are there only ransacking mercenaries running loose on this island?"

"Because it is a test for us."

"A test? Of what kind?"

"The winner gets a high-paying opportunity. You know how this all works."

"Once I did. But no longer. I'm taking you in Danton. You and the rest of these guys."

"I can't allow that." Maveth replied, raising his gun.

As the two stood off, Gunbaine bolted in the room, quickly seeing Henshaw, who's gaze turned toward him as did his gun.

"Seriously." Gunbaine said.

"Smalls!" Henshaw replied. "You too? What's going on here?!"

"I've already explained it, Marshall." Maveth said. "Put down your weapon and let us be."

"As I've already stated, I cannot allow that."

Gunbaine fired a shot toward Henshaw. Maveth shoved Gunbaine as the fire didn't impact Henshaw, who moved to the other side of the room, diving down. Gunbaine fell to the floor, looking up toward Maveth.

"The hell was that for?!"

"He doesn't need to die." Maveth clarified. "Believe me, he's not worth the kill."

Maveth helped Gunbaine to his feet and the two mercenaries left the room right as Henshaw stood up. He saw them leave and shook his head. Henshaw went ahead and contacted the agents who were still in the mansion to keep their eyes open for Maveth and Gunbaine. Maveth and Gunbaine ran down the hall, reaching the front room of the mansion. They stopped. No signs of agents or the other mercenaries.

"We're the only ones left?" Gunbaine questioned.

"I doubt that."

They quickly hear pacing steps coming from behind them. Once they turned to look, they saw Tessa running. She ran right into them, standing next to Maveth, leaving Gunbaine in a moment of confusion. Tessa pointed down the hall where she had come.

"They're following me."

"Who's following you?" Gunbaine asked.

"I have an idea." Maveth noted, seeing Lynch and Kane in their sights.

"Shit, looks like they're still alive." Lynch said.

"No issue for us." Kane replied. "We can deal with them easily and leave the girl for ourselves."

Maveth placed his gun back into his holster and pulled out his sword. Gunbaine stood firm with his weapons loaded and ready. Tessa exhaled as she took out her staff. Lynch and Kane laughed, mocking the three. Lynch reached toward his back, revealing he had a staff of his own. One used for hunting.

"Let's get this over with." Lynch said.

IV

HIS MARK SCORCHES

Lynch and Kane rushed toward Maveth, Gunbaine, and Tessa as the fight began. Maveth used his sword against Lynch's hunting staff. Kane fired shots at Gunbaine while Tessa lunged at him with her staff, Kane dodged the incoming blow and continued shooting toward Gunbaine. The two fired back at one another continuously with Tessa dodging in between the gunfight. Maveth and Lynch continued their bout with the sword and staff. Lynch shoved Maveth to the wall and pressed him against it with the end of the staff on his chest. Maveth grunted as he pushed Lynch back.

"You can't win this game." Lynch said. "This is my time."

"Only if you can make your way out of this mansion still on your feet."

Lynch went for a left kick toward Maveth's right knee, et, Maveth's reflexes were too quick for Lynch to connect the attack and Maveth swiped his sword against Lynch's leg, slashing him as the blood seeped out. Lynch limped stepping back with Maveth moving forward. Lynch swiped the staff to avoid Maveth's incoming close range. However, the Death-Bringer stopped and looked over toward Tessa.

"Balthazar!" Maveth yelled.

Kane punched Gunbaine and Tessa moved over, tripping the Mercenary with her staff. As she had done that action, she heard Maveth calling her name. Glancing over, seeing Lynch holding his leg in pain with Maveth signaling her to come over with his finger. Tessa went over and stood next to Maveth, looking in disgust toward Lynch.

"Best you have the last hit." Maveth said.

"You can't kill me!" Lynch yelled. "Those are the rules of this game. I am to be still alive when this is all over!"

"Yes, I cannot kill you." Tessa replied. "But, I can hurt you. Hurt you enough to remember it was me who eliminated you from the game."

Lynch scoffed, rubbing the blood from his leg onto his hand and swiping it in the faces of both Maveth and Tess. Maveth rushed at him with the sword, set to impale him in the chest, but Tessa stopped him. His anger could get the better of him and she could sense it. She nodded and Maveth knew as he looked over, seeing Gunbaine and Kane now in a fistfight.

"Take care of him." Maveth told Tessa. "And help us with this last one."

"Will do." Tessa smiled.

Maveth ran over to assist Gunbaine while Tessa looked down at Lynch with her staff gripped. Lynch laughed.

"If only you let us have our way. This shit could've been much different."

"It's where it needs to be. If I ever see you again outside of this game, I will kill you."

"Will you now?"

"Don't tempt me otherwise."

"Piss off!"

Tessa smacked the staff across Lynch's head, knocking him unconscious. Afterwards, she turned to see Maveth and Gunbaine against Kane and ran over to help them.

On the second floor, Henshaw regrouped with the remaining

agents as they prepared an ambush on the first floor. Henshaw sought to take out Maveth, Gunbaine, and Tessa by any means. However, as he and the agents walked down the hall, the exchange Force was waiting on them. Their armor glared with the incoming sunlight of the dusk.

"Fire!" Henshaw yelled.

The agents let out their rounds toward the Force, but their armor was too dense for their bullets to penetrate. Something Henshaw is familiar with. He stomped his foot, commanding the agents to return to the helicopter outside. Once the agents made a move to evacuate, the Force came at them with attacks from all corners. Henshaw ran and as he continued running, he ran right into Cain. Henshaw raised his head, looking up at the brute figure.

"I have no quarrel with you." Cain said. "Leave the Exchange Force to me."

"Bit, you're a mercenary. I have to bring you in."

"Leave." Cain commanded. "Or else this mansion shall be your grave."

Henshaw nodded in agreement, he ran down the hall, eventually entering the front room seeing Maveth, Gunbaine, and Tessa fighting against Kane the Mercenary. Maveth looked and saw Henshaw. He pointed down the hallway as other agents came running past him to the outside.

"He's coming!" Henshaw told Maveth. "Prepare yourselves!"

"Who's coming?" Maveth questioned.

Henshaw and the remaining agents entered the helicopter and left the mansion grounds. On the second floor, the Force finished killing the agents who could not escape. The leading member heard the fighting downstairs.

"We must go and end this game."

Once the Force took a step toward the steps, Cain was already there. Breathing calmer than most. The Force stood their ground, posed for the fight. Cain was already prepared. No need to put his arms up or to make a stance. His posture of standing still was enough to project fear into his opponents.

"Forgot about you." A member said. "This will be challenging."

"You must remember. My mark scorches all who come into my path. This day, you five have done so."

"Bring it, big man!"

The Force jumped on Cain, attacking him from every corner they could find. Cain shoved them back, grabbing the lean member of the Force and smashing him into the floor, causing the entire floor to tremble. Downstairs, dust fell fro steeling, gaining Maveth's attention. Tessa also saw the dust and could hear the loud bangs from above.

"What was that?" She wondered.

"Trouble." Maveth said. "And it's coming our way."

Cain fought the remaining four, taking them out with slams into the floor, the walls, and the ceiling. He left the leader last. The leader was as big in size as Cain. A perfect match of sorts, one Cain preferred in fights. The leader punched Cain several times in the face before Cain grabbed him by his throat, ripping his armor from his body and throwing him off the balcony as he fell to the first floor. Gunbaine kicked Kane the Mercenary near the balcony as the body fell next to him. The fight had paused as they each looked up toward the second floor and could hear the loud footsteps coming down from the stairs.

"Oh shit." Gunbaine uttered.

"I know." Maveth said. "I know."

Kane himself turned around as the footsteps reached the first floor and now to their knowledge, Maveth looked outside to find it was now nightfall and Cain was standing in the room.

Gunbaine raised his glocks and Tessa had her staff ready. Maveth stood still, watching the room and everyone who was in it. It clicked into his mind. This is all who is left of the game. Deadon is eliminated. So is Bandit and even the Exchange Force. it was now down to the five to see who would become the victor of Marion's game. Cain had stood over Kane the Mercenary, who walked up to him, staring at him.

"So, we share a common name." Kane said. "How about you and I team up to take these guys out. Leave the game to ourselves?"

"No." Cain said.

"If you say so…" Kane raised up his gun and went to fire it, but Cain grabbed his arm, breaking it as he lifted him up. Kane screamed in pain, dropping the gun from his hand.

"You are too weak." Cain said.

Cain tossed Kane the Mercenary out of the window to the outside. He turned, seeing Maveth, Gunbaine, and Tessa. He walked toward them very, very slowly.

"It is now the four of us." Cain said. "I will take care of you swiftly and collect whatever the prize may be."

"We will not back down!" Gunbaine yelled. "You hear me!"

"Surrender isn't something we're used to." Tessa added. "I'm sure you know that."

Cain nodded.

"I respect your decisions."

Cain quickly moved like a bull toward them, shoving Maveth into the wall as he grabbed Gunbaine by his head and threw him outside of a window. Tessa ran at him with the staff, hitting his legs, arms, and neck. Cain shrugged the attacks off and backhanded Tessa to the ground. Maveth stood up, seeing Tessa down and Gunbaine outside. He set his focus on Cain.

"I knocked you back for a reason." Cain said.

"And that reason is?"

"You're the one I wanted to meet. The famed Death-Bringer."

"Well, today's your fucking damn day."

Cain chucked under the mask.

"I've always wanted to know what it was like to defeat a man of your caliber. You've come across many warriors who could match you."

"I have. Most of them are dead."

"Well, we'll see how this day turns out."

Cain posed himself, ready for the fight. Maveth took the moment to think. He saw that Cain had no weapons in hand. Maveth's a fair guy. He raised one of his guns toward Cain. Cain waved it off.

"I have no need for firearms or swords or staves. My hands are enough. My feet are enough. I am enough."

Maveth set down his weapons. All of them and stood up facing Cain with his fists balled up, his feet in position. Cain nodded.

"Now you're thinking like a true fighter."

"Only one way to see who's the true fighter." Maveth said. "What are you waiting for?"

▼

THE DEATH-BRINGER VS. THE CURSE

Cain moved like a raging bull toward Maveth, ramming him into the wall of the room. Maveth kicked, punched, and uppercutted Cain as he held him. The wall cracked from the impact. Maveth double-kicked Cain back and he ran toward the big man, jumping over his head and hitting Cain with a roundhouse kick. Cain stumbled and turned around slowly toward Maveth. Cain shrugged himself.

"You're good." Cain uttered. "You have skill."

"I have a lot more in me."

"I see that."

Cain lunged over, pummeling Maveth in the chest and stomach with his fist. Maveth fell to his hands and knees from the attacks as Cain stomped him in the back. Maveth held himself up as the foot crashed atop his back, right in the middle. Maveth did not let out a noise of pain. He took it in, shoving Cain back before delivering a series of jabs to Cain's face and a head butt. Cain backed up with several steps and Maveth ran toward him, spearing him against the wall. On the floor, Tessa's eyes opened, what she saw Maveth and Cain going at it. Too hurt to raise up and help him, Tessa's eyes closed.

Cain grabbed Maveth by his neck, slamming him into the floor and dragging him across the room. Cain raised the

Death-Bringer up to his feet and tossed him outside through one of the remaining windows. Maveth rolled across the ground. He picked himself up before seeing the downed Gunbaine beside him. Gunbaine still lives, he's only knocked out. Maveth could tell by hearing Gunbaine's calm pulse. Cain walked out from the front doors, moving toward Maveth.

"They say you are the Death-Bringer." Cain spoke. "The Slayer of Heroes. I must know to be certain, are you truly who they claim you to be? Or are you just another man with a title yet to be claimed?"

Maveth stood up, stumbling on his feet. He faced down Cain as his helmet is shattered and cracked across the eyes. Maveth removed his helment, revealing his face toward Cain. Cain saw how young Maveth was, from there Cain knew how much experience and knowledge he possessed. Enough to match a fifty-year old veteran in the force. Cain stomped the ground, shaking it to cause Maveth to stumble once more in his place. Maveth did not stumble. He held himself together.

"Answer my question." Cain said. "Are you who they claim you to be?"

"I claim to be only a man on a mission." Maveth said. "A man looking for his next duty. A man who will stop at nothing to accomplish a task. Any task. Who am I? I am Danton Thomas to those who call me friend or brother. To the world, I am Maveth, The Death-Bringer. The Slayer of Heroes."

Cain applauded. Showing some respect for Maveth. However, it did not matter as Cain speared Maveth into the ground. The dirt flying upwards and landing on Maveth's face. Cain stood over him. His eyes glaring red and his breathing deep. He placed his right foot atop Maveth's chest. Maveth fought back, punching Cain's knee and leg. The attacks did not faze him. For his leg was too large to be harmed from Maveth's punches.

"It appears I cannot kill you, Death-Bringer. Much like the

others out here. I can only leave you all in a deep sleep. Only to be awoken to a defeated dream. That is the fate of your kind. All will know of your fates and they will understand the curse has been sealed."

Maveth exhaled. Looking Cain in the eyes.

"Fuck your curse."

Maveth rolled himself from Cain's foot as he collapsed to the ground. Cain swiped toward Maveth, yet he ducked under the attack and punched Cain in the throat. Cain paused, holding is neck and stepped back. Maveth looked on and continued his punches, kicks, and attacks on Cain. Wearing the big man down. Cain stumbled and fell to one knee. Maveth ran and double-kicked Cain in the face, cracking his mask and Cain fell down. Maveth stood over him and started pummeling Cain in the face with sharp punches. He continued the attacks until he heard the sound of a helicopter approaching. Maveth ceased the attacks and looked up to the night sky, only to see a V.A.U.L.T. helicopter landing. Maveth walked away from Cain toward the helicopter, seeing Marion stepping off and approaching him. Marion looked around at the mansion. Seeing the broken windows and the bodies of the agents and mercenaries in her sight. She chuckled.

"I take it this was eventful."

"The game's over. I've won."

Marion looked behind Maveth, seeing Cain on the ground, slowly moving. Cain went to raise himself up yet fell back to the ground. Marion shook her head as Maveth nodded, wiping the blood from his face.

"You didn't tell me you owned this island."

"And why would I have done that?"

"No reason."

"Looks like it was a tough one." Marion said. "However, you got through it. Alive and well."

"Appearing can be altering if you're not aware of the causes."

"You have kept up yours in a manner of sorts. None of the mercenaries appear to have been killed. The game is over. You've won, Danton."

"So, what's next?"

"You go home. I will contact you regarding the prize. I'm sure it will take to your liking."

After some time, the mercenaries were all gathered by V.A.U.L.T. and returned to their primary areas. Cain had disappeared from the mansion grounds, unable to be found. Danton returned to his home and rested. Several days had passed and Danton received a phone call from Marion, telling him to meet her at the headquarters. Same office as usual.

Danton traveled to the headquarters and entered Marion's office. Yet, this time she was not alone. Sir Onyx and Kex Kendrick were also present in the office. Danton was caught off guard and Marion calmed him in his slow uncertainty of appearances.

"They are here for you."

"For me? I've already worked with Onyx. But, Kex Kendrick. I am not familiar with his methods."

"But you've heard of me?"

"I have. Many who have paid for my services have mentioned you by name. claiming your goals for this world are far out there. Some have called you a psychotic."

"That's only a word replaceable for a genius mind."

"Why are the two of you here?"

"They are here because of the prize." Marion said.

"The prize? What is it? Money? Gold? An island to call my own?"

"It is something much more valuable." Sir Onyx replied.

"Something you crave deeply in your soul."

"You better not be wasting my time."

"We're not." Kex said. "Onyx, tell him of the prize. Your side of it, at least."

"His side?"

Onyx grabbed a file which was sitting on Marion's desk and handed it to Danton. He opened it and saw what was inside. Danton's eyes widen, gazing up at the file and Onyx.

"Is this true?"

"It is." Marion said. "Onyx isn't the only one who has one to show you."

Kex handed Danton a file of his own. Danton opened it and saw the details inside. He looked up to Kex.

"You wish me to face him?"

"You defeated the mercenaries. I'm sure you can handle the titagod."

Danton closed the file and set it down on the corner of the desk next to him. Kex nodded, glaring at Danton and the file folder.

"Another time." Danton said. "However, this one I am interested in."

"Figured you would be." Onyx replied. "I always knew you were looking for a rematch."

Danton closed the file, grabbing it and Kex's file. He turned toward Marion and she nodded with a grin.

"I'll take the tasks. These are truly prizes to behold for a mercenary such as myself."

"Are you sure you're ready for this?" Marion asked. "After what you've been through, can you handle another set of bouts? Is it any good for your health?"

"I'm with the lady on this one." Kex added. "Can you complete the contracts you've been given?"

"Kex, do not doubt the man." Onyx said. "He's proven to me

he can accomplish anything that comes in his way. I trust in him and his skill set.”

“How soon shall I get started?” Danton asked.

“How soon can you get there?” Marion asked.

“I’m on my way now.” Danton replied. “Thank you for this opportunity.”

Danton stopped in his steps and turned back to Marion.

“I must know. How’s Tessa?”

“The huntress? She is doing well. Already on another treasure hunt last I was told.”

“Good to know.”

“What’s it to you?” Kex asked. “She an old lover or something?”

“Something else. Reminds me of something else.”

Danton left the office with the files. In his truck, he placed the file which Kex gave him down in the seat and opened the file from Onyx. He grinned as he read the details and saw the photo of the target. A silhouette of a figure moving through the city. Carrying with it a sword. He savored the opportunity and the coming moments ahead.

“We meet again, *Myth-Walker.*”

THE SERIES WILL CONTINUE IN...

MAVETH

VS.

THE SWORDMAN

ABOUT THE AUTHOR

Ty'Ron W. C. Robinson II is the author of several works of fiction. Including the *Dark Titan Universe Saga* series (*Dark Titan Knights, The Resistance Protocol, Tales of the Scattered, Tales of the Numinous, Day of Octagon*) and *The Haunted City Saga* series. Also of other books (*Lost in Shadows, Hod, The Book of The Elect, Symbolum Venatores, etc.*) and One-Shot short stories More information pertaining to the author and stories can be found at darktitanentertainment.com.

Twitter: @TyronRobinsonII
Instagram: @tyronrobinsonii

Twitter: @DarkTitan_
Instagram: @darktitanentertainment

www.ingramcontent.com/pod-product-compliance
Lightning Source LLC
Chambersburg PA
CBHW050900130726
47900CB00013B/755